WRIN

by
Jerry Spinelli

Student Packet
Written by
Elizabeth M. Klar
and Cheryl Klar-Trim

Contains masters for:

2 Prereading Activities
1 Study Guide (8 pages)
10 Vocabulary Activities
3 Critical Thinking Activities
3 Literary Analysis Activities
2 Writing Activities
1 Art Activity
2 Comprehension Quizzes
1 Novel Test (5 pages)

Plus   Detailed Answer Key

> ### Note
> The paperback text used to prepare this guide was published by HarperCollins Publishers, Inc. ©1997 by Jerry Spinelli. The page references may differ in other editions.
>
> **Please note:** Please assess the appropriateness of this book for the age level and maturity of your students prior to reading and discussing it with your class.

ISBN 1-58130-677-6

Directions: Rate each of the following statements before you read the novel and discuss your ratings with a partner. After you have completed the novel, rate and discuss the statements again.

1 ———— 2 ———— 3 ———— 4 ———— 5 ———— 6
strongly agree   strongly disagree

	Before	**After**
1. The adults in the family are always right.	_____	_____
2. Children should never ask questions when their parents tell them to do something.	_____	_____
3. Wishes never come true.		
4. A true friend never teases or hurts you.	_____	_____
5. People always change for the better as they get older.	_____	_____
6. Mothers and fathers always do what is best for their children.	_____	_____
7. You should always do what your peers tell you to do.	_____	_____
8. Younger children have nothing to teach older people.	_____	_____
9. People can disagree and still love and trust each other.	_____	_____
10. Children cannot make decisions for themselves.	_____	_____
11. If things get too hard to do, you should just give up.	_____	_____
12. It's important to like and accept yourself.	_____	_____
13. You should always keep your promises.	_____	_____
14. Good intentions are always helpful.	_____	_____
15. To succeed, you must keep trying to solve the problem.	_____	_____

Directions: Think about each idea listed below, then freewrite about each one for at least five minutes. Use extra paper if you need it. Be prepared to discuss your thoughts with classmates.

1. family

2. loyalty

3. friendship

4. birthday

5. wishes

6. peer pressure

7. love

8. pets

9. hunting

4

Name _____

Section One, Chapters 1-4
1. What is the first thing Palmer learns about himself?
2. What is the moment Palmer dreads above all others?
3. What is a wringer?
4. What does Beans do to Palmer's birthday cake?
5. Who does Palmer say is the boss of all the kids in the neighborhood under ten years old?
6. What do Beans, Mutto, and Henry give Palmer for his birthday?
7. What nickname do Beans, Mutto, and Henry give Palmer?
8. Who is the tallest of Palmer's friends?
9. Who is Fishface?
10. What do the boys leave on Dorothy's top step? What do they hope she will think it is?
11. How does Palmer feel about the park? Why?
12. What excuse does Palmer give his friends for not playing with them on the soccer field?
13. Who does Palmer think is the meekest of the group?
14. What is Palmer reminded of as he watches his friends pretending to be wringers?

Section Two, Chapters 5-8
1. What are the boys doing when Palmer catches up with them at the playground?
2. What does Beans want to do when Palmer catches up with them?
3. What does Beans do to the other boys the first time he is on the bottom of the stack?
4. How does Beans react when a lady on the playground yells, "Hey, you kids, no stacking"?
5. Who is Farquar?
6. What is The Treatment? What specifically does Farquar do to Palmer?
7. What do Beans and Mutto do as Palmer receives The Treatment?
8. How does Mr. LaRue's opinion of Beans differ from his wife's?
9. Where does Beans' nickname come from?
10. What does Palmer's dad give him for his birthday?
11. Where does Palmer hide the gift his father gives him?

5

12. What does Palmer do to keep from thinking about his aching arm?

13. What is Palmer doing when he begins crying inconsolably?

14. Is Palmer happy when his arm starts to heal? Why?

15. How does Dorothy treat Palmer when he tries to talk to her and show her his bruises?

16. What does Palmer find befuddling about the way Dorothy behaves as he and his friends make fun of her?

17. What does Palmer think is the worst day of the year? Why?

18. What is one of the many questions about Pigeon Day that bewilders Palmer?

19. How old was Palmer on his first Pigeon Day?

20. What does Palmer pretend the words on the pigeon statue say?

21. Was Palmer's father a wringer when he was a boy?

22. Does Mr. LaRue want Palmer to be a wringer?

Section Three, Chapters 9-12

1. With whom does Palmer attend the second Pigeon Day?

2. Who does Palmer explain Pigeon Day to?

3. How does Dorothy react to Palmer's explanation of what is going to happen to the birds on Pigeon Day?

4. Who is Arthur Dodds?

5. What are Dorothy and Palmer doing instead of going to Pigeon Day?

6. What does Arthur Dodds do with the pigeon he wrings?

7. What does Palmer smell as he sits on his father's lap?

8. Who is Billy Natola?

9. What excuse do Beans and Mutto give Palmer for why he can't join their gang?

10. What does Mrs. LaRue do when no one shows up for Palmer's eighth birthday party?

11. Why does Palmer think the pigeon looks like a most agreeable bird?

12. How does Palmer discover that his father is a shooter?

13. When did Palmer discover that he did not want to be a wringer?

14. What does Mr. LaRue say is the reason for Pigeon Day?

15. What does Palmer plan to do so he doesn't have to meet the gang at the cannon on Pigeon Day?

16. Who sneaks into Palmer's house as he has his nightmare about the pigeons dropping the town into the sun?

17. Where do the boys go on their midnight outing?

18. What does Palmer do instead of going to the pigeon shoot?

Section Four, Chapters 13-16

1. What does Mr. LaRue say happens whenever he decides not to take an umbrella?

2. What happens to the weather after Palmer puts his sled in the basement?

3. What does Palmer do during the snow day?

4. What or who does Palmer find tapping on his bedroom window in the morning before school?

5. Who do Palmer and the gang attack with snowballs on their way to school?

6. Does Palmer feel better the night when the pigeon isn't sitting on his windowsill anymore?

7. What does Palmer think is the reason the bird is tapping on the window?

8. What does Palmer feed the bird?

9. How does the bird behave as it walks into Palmer's room?

10. How do the pigeon's toes feel on Palmer's head?

11. After looking at the bird from behind, does Palmer think the bird is starving? Why?

12. How does Mrs. LaRue react when Palmer asks her to knock before entering his room?

13. Why does Mrs. LaRue think Palmer wants her to knock before entering his room?

Section Five, Chapters 17-20

1. How does the pigeon awaken Palmer in the morning?

2. What does Palmer bring the bird to eat in addition to the FrankenPuffs?

3. Does Palmer have to coax the bird to eat the cereal?

4. What does Palmer sneak out of the library?

5. What does "roosting" mean?

6. What does Palmer learn about the eating habits of pigeons from reading a book?

7. In addition to it being the size of an acorn, what does Palmer learn about a pigeon's heart?

8. Why does Palmer name the bird Nipper?

9. What is the hardest part of Palmer's new routine with Nipper?

10. What does Palmer do to make his mother ask, "Is this another sign of your maturity?"

11. Why does Palmer use Dorothy as a diversion?

12. What is treestumping?

13. What kind of house does Palmer imagine Beans lives in?

14. What kind of house does Beans really live in?

15. What does Beans have hidden in a frozen spaghetti dinner in his freezer?

16. What does Palmer think the muskrat body looks like?

17. Where did Beans get the muskrat?

18. What does Henry tell Palmer about Panther?

19. What does Beans do with the muskrat?

20. Who finds the dead muskrat at the Gruziks' house?

21. What does Mutto claim to see in the sky right after the muskrat incident?

Section Six, Chapters 21-24

1. What does Beans chase after near Palmer's house?

2. What does Palmer do to distract his friends from the pigeon sighting?

3. What made this day tense and uncomfortable?

4. What does Palmer do to Nipper as soon as he comes tapping on the window?

5. What are some of the things Palmer wonders if Nipper does during the day?

6. What does Palmer know he should wish about Nipper?

7. How do the boys treat Dorothy after the muskrat incident?

8. What do the school kids do after noticing how much fun Palmer and his friends have treestumping Dorothy?

9. What piece of clothing does Beans keep taking from Dorothy?

10. What does Dorothy do that finally makes Palmer think of her as a person and not as a target?

11. Who does Palmer think has hurt Dorothy the most, Beans or himself?

12. How does Palmer react when Nipper fails to come home?

13. To whom does Palmer reveal his secret about Nipper?

14. What are the gifts Beans receives from Palmer, Mutto, and Henry on his tenth birthday?

15. Why does Beans want to get The Treatment?

16. Does Beans give any indication that his arm hurts after receiving The Treatment?

17. Who are the Beans Boys?

18. How does Dorothy get Nipper to sit on her head?

19. What swimming term does Palmer use to describe the way Dorothy makes him feel?

20. What does Palmer tell Dorothy about wanting to be a wringer?

21. How does Dorothy respond to Palmer's news about being a wringer?

22. What does Palmer think Beans will do to him if he isn't a wringer?

23. How does Palmer react when Dorothy kisses him?

Section Seven, Chapters 25-28

1. What happens to Palmer to make him feel as if he has fallen into a black hole?

2. How does Palmer react when Nipper lands on his head as he walks with his friends?

3. How does Palmer claim, to his friends, he feels about pigeons?

4. What are the two words Palmer does not want Dorothy to say out loud in front of Nipper?

5. What does Dorothy write on Palmer's Nerf ball?

6. What does Palmer do the next day to keep Nipper from recognizing him on his way to and from school?

7. What is the bad thing Palmer tells his teacher he has done?

8. What punishment does the teacher assign to Palmer?

9. What is the reason Palmer gives his friends for why he is wearing his winter clothes?

10. Which member of the gang is the only one who occasionally calls Palmer by his real name?

11. What are the two problems Palmer faces each morning as he leaves the house?

12. What does he do to solve both of his problems?

13. What does Palmer tell his teacher is the reason he has been acting up in school?

14. What does Palmer do to make his popularity soar at school and give him the reputation for being a kid who does crazy things?

15. What does Palmer plan to wear to school on the last day? Why?

16. What kind of school does the gang take Palmer to?

17. What color is the wringmaster's cap?

18. How many shots does the wringmaster say each shooter gets?

19. What does the wringmaster say is the magic word?

20. What are "floppers"?

21. What is special about August seven?

Section Eight, Chapters 29-32

1. What were Dorothy and Palmer playing with as Nipper looked down from his perch on the curtain rod?

2. What does Dorothy tell Palmer to say to everybody?

3. How is Palmer's social life divided?

4. What is Palmer's strategy for surviving the summer?

5. What is a wish that Palmer sometimes makes?

6. Where does Palmer's mother see the yellow cat?

7. What are the boys thrilled about when they go to Palmer's birthday party?

8. What does Palmer see in the shimmering shapes of the candle flames?

9. Can Palmer and the gang find Farquar for The Treatment?

10. What does Palmer find on his leftover birthday cake?

11. How many times does Beans climb Palmer's stairs during the birthday party?

12. Where does Palmer decide to hide that night?

13. What happens to Nipper when he settles down to roost?

14. What does Palmer forget in his closet?

15. Who rings the doorbell early the next morning before Palmer eats breakfast?

16. Where does Palmer say he spent the night?

17. Who does Beans tell Palmer they have to go see?

18. What is Farquar eating when the gang meets him in front of the deli?

19. What does Palmer say when Farquar tells Palmer to roll up his sleeve?

20. What happens after Palmer refuses to take The Treatment?

Section Nine, Chapters 33-36

1. Where does Palmer hide from Beans?

2. What kind of drink does the worker from the GreatGrocer give to Palmer?

3. When does Palmer make a run for his house?

4. What is sitting on Palmer's pillow looking at Nipper on the windowsill?

5. Where does Dorothy suggest that Palmer hide Nipper?

6. Do Dorothy and Palmer really want Nipper gone? Why or why not?

7. What does Dorothy find in the street?

8. What do Palmer and Dorothy take with them on their journey besides Nipper?

9. What does Dorothy feed Nipper when she and Palmer stop to eat?

10. Where does Palmer finally let Nipper go?

11. What do Palmer and Dorothy buy at the gas station?

12. What do Palmer and Dorothy find as they enter Palmer's bedroom?

13. Who comes into Palmer's bedroom after breakfast?

14. What does Palmer's mother tell him?

15. What does Palmer's mother use to clean the dropping from the desk?

16. Where is Dorothy going on vacation?

17. What does Palmer ask Dorothy to do on her vacation?

18. Who inspects Palmer's bedroom?

19. What is Henry's real name?

20. What does Palmer ask Henry to tell the gang?

Section Ten, Chapters 37-40

1. Where does Palmer ride his bike?

2. Where does Palmer keep his soldiers after he throws away the shoebox?

3. What skill does Mr. LaRue teach Palmer?

4. Where does Palmer put his toy soldiers after his battle with the eraser is won?

5. Where do Palmer and his father go to see the Titans baseball game?

6. What important event happens at the Titans baseball game?

7. What does Palmer imagine he feels as he holds the foul ball his father gave him?

8. What are the men and women doing to get ready for the town's celebration?

9. What does Palmer dream about one night?

10. Name Palmer's favorite pie at the Family Fest.

11. What does Palmer's father do this year at the Family Fest that he had not done in years past?

12. Where does Palmer ride his bike on Friday?

13. What does Palmer find at the train station?

14. How many birds do the white boxes hold?

15. What jobs do Beans, Mutto, and Henry have at the Family Fest?

16. Who does Palmer meet at the Family Fest?

17. Where does Dorothy tell Palmer she let Nipper go?

18. Who runs away from Palmer screaming? Why?

19. Who tells Palmer that he must leave the stack of pigeon crates?

20. What does one shooter aim and shoot at instead of a pigeon?

21. Who does Palmer talk to at the edge of the shooting field?

22. Who takes Nipper to the center of the field and slams him to the ground?

23. How does Palmer save his pigeon from being killed?

rural (1)	frolicking (1)	climax (1)	punctured (3)
grub (6)	cackled (7)	piped (8)	crusty (8)
wick (10)	hoodlums (11)	booted (12)	rumbled (12)
smirk (12)	cringed (13)	veered (16)	lurched (16)
tilted (16)	meekest (17)	careening (17)	woozy (18)
hovered (18)			

Directions: Write each vocabulary word on a slip of paper (one word per piece). Using the circle below, make a spinner. Now play the following game with a classmate. (It is a good idea to have a dictionary and thesaurus handy.) Place the papers in a small container. The first player draws a word from the container. The player then spins the spinner and follows the direction where the pointer lands. For example, if the player draws the word "smirk" and lands on "define," the player must define the word "smirk". If the player's partner accepts the answer as correct, the first player scores one point and play passes to the second player. If the player's partner challenges the answer, the first player uses a dictionary or thesaurus to prove the answer is correct. If the player can prove the answer is correct, the player earns two points. If the player cannot prove the answer is correct, the opposing player earns two points. Play continues until all the words have been used. The player with the most points is the winner.

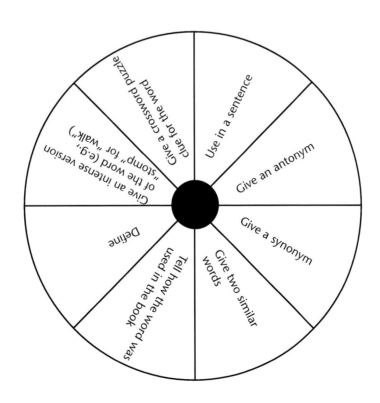

legendary (20)	ultimate (21)	zombies (21)	hotfoot (23)
bashed (25)	gravely (26)	daintily (27)	bluntly (28)
warpath (28)	tingled (31)	boulevard (33)	squeamish (33)
diminishing (34)	taunt (36)	befuddled (36)	bewildered (39)
spewing (39)	hobbling (39)	etched (42)	teeming (42)

Directions: Choose ten words from the vocabulary list. On a separate sheet of paper, make a word map (like the one shown below) for each word.

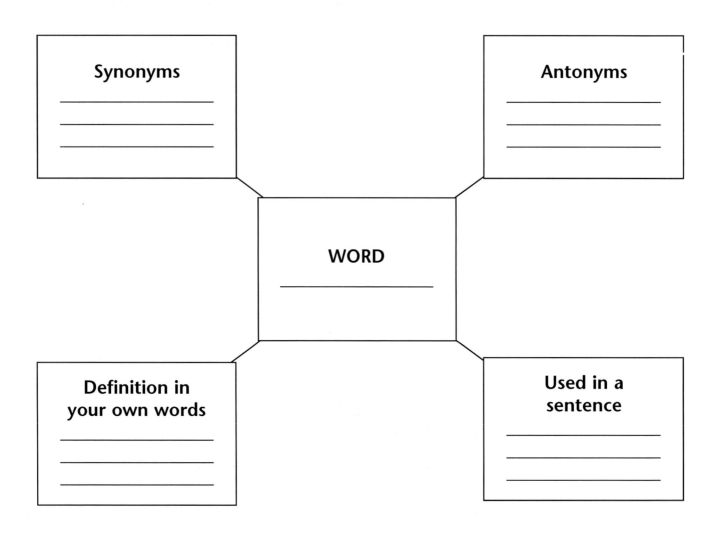

© Novel Units, Inc.

14

clueing (44)	smugly (44)	misery (46)	dashing (47)
bronco (48)	nuisance (48)	nuzzled (50)	tourist (51)
strutted (51)	smothered (52)	cooing (53)	wobbled (56)
bazookas (57)	intended (58)	fiery (59)	yanked (60)
skirting (61)	snagged (62)	taffy (62)	wrenching (63)
uproar (63)			

Directions: Read each word below. The first letter of a related vocabulary word appears after each word. The related word may be either a synonym or an antonym. Write the related vocabulary word on the line. Look at each word pair. If the two words are synonyms, write "s" to the left of the question. If they are antonyms, write "a" on the line to the left.

___ 1. jerk - y_____

___ 2. pleasure - n_____

___ 3. chaos - u_____

___ 4. planned - I_____

___ 5. chilly - f_____

___ 6. sway - w_____

___ 7. rushing - d_____

___ 8. slink - s_____

___ 9. comfortable - m_____

___ 10. twist - w_____

doozie (67)   blizzard (67)   classic (67)   Maserati (67)
adiós (68)   flakes (68)   grumped (69)   syrupy (69)
lobbed (71)   replying (72)   restraint (73)   concentrating (74)
plunged (74)   groggies (76)   persuader (77)   yelped (80)
scrap (80)   ambled (83)   swooped (83)   giggly (84)

Directions: Cut a nine-inch square out of white construction paper. Fold paper in half diagonally (from corner to corner). Unfold paper. Fold the paper in half again (Figure A). Then cut one fold from the outer corner to the center of the paper (Figure B). Slide one cut piece on top of the other to form a triangular shape with a base and two standing sides. Glue the pieces together (Figure C). On the inside base, write a vocabulary word. On the inside left, write a sentence using the vocabulary word. On the inside right, draw a picture to illustrate the vocabulary word. Repeat the process for at least nine words from the list. Glue the back sides of your completed triangles together and hang them as a mobile.

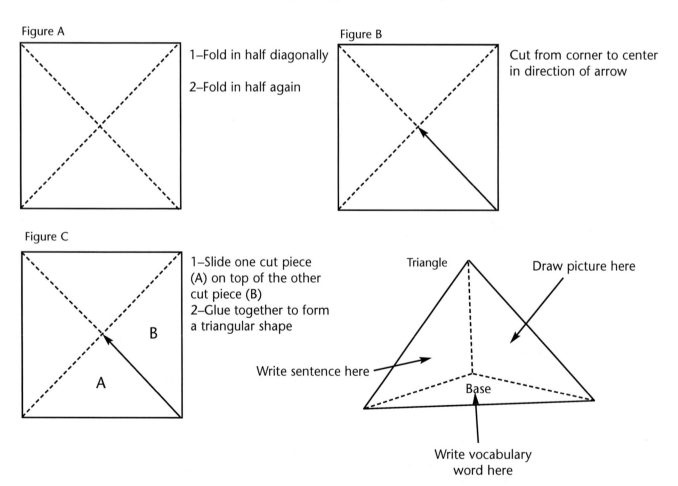

Figure A

1–Fold in half diagonally

2–Fold in half again

Figure B

Cut from corner to center in direction of arrow

Figure C

1–Slide one cut piece (A) on top of the other cut piece (B)
2–Glue together to form a triangular shape

B

A

Triangle

Draw picture here

Write sentence here

Base

Write vocabulary word here

earlobe (88)	nooks (90)	crannies (90)	skids (92)
routine (93)	stupendous (94)	maturity (95)	mushy (95)
scenarios (96)	cooties (96)	infested (97)	divert (97)
lean-to (99)	chime (99)	primitive (99)	recoiled (100)
flotsam (101)	Technicolor (102)	buckshot (104)	boundless (104)

Directions: Write a cinquain poem choosing the vocabulary words from chapters 17-20.

A cinquain is a simple five-line poem about one subject. One format is as follows:

Line 1 = the title [one word]

Line 2 = description of the title [two words]

Line 3 = expression of action [three words]

Line 4 = expression of feeling [four words]

Line 5 = a synonym for the title [one word]

_____

_____

_____

_____

_____

Name _____

scanned (105)	deli (106)	prim (106)	reluctant (108)
carcass (108)	consequences (108)	scowl (109)	multicolored (110)
flinched (110)	spectators (111)	smoldered (111)	silhouette (113)
roosting (114)	raucous (119)	gobs (119)	dilemma (120)
clusters (121)	registered (121)	cackling (123)	phooey (125)
snickered (130)			

Directions: Your teacher will divide the class into two teams, giving each team a stack of notecards with vocabulary words on them. A member of team #1 will look at a card and read it silently. Then he/she will go in front of the class and pantomime the vocabulary word. Team #2 will try to guess the vocabulary word. The teams take turns acting out vocabulary words for each other. The teacher will assign one point each time a vocabulary word is guessed correctly. Continue with the game until all cards have been used. After the game, collect the cards and put them in a stack. Each member of the team should then draw a vocabulary card from the stack and write a sentence using the word he or she chooses. Share your sentences with the class.

consequences

bugle (132)	snipped (133)	crouched (134)	paced (136)
agitated (136)	tittered (137)	disguise (138)	anticipated (140)
mobbed (143)	detain (145)	immensely (146)	egged (146)
morsels (147)	spouted (147)	walloped (151)	rasped (151)
leering (152)	piped (153)	humanely (156)	jeers (157)

Directions: Select ten vocabulary words from above. Create a crossword puzzle answer key by filling in the grid below. Be sure to number the squares for each word. Blacken any spaces not used by the letters. Then, write clues to the crossword puzzle. Number the clues to match the numbers in the squares. The teacher will give each student a blank grid. Make a blank copy of your crossword puzzle for other students to answer. Exchange your clues with someone else and solve the blank puzzle he/she gives you. Check the completed puzzles with answer keys.

impish (160)	sagged (160)	strategy (161)	traitor (161)
dopey (162)	waddling (163)	thrilled (164)	shimmering (166)
devastated (166)	smeared (168)	put out (169)	nacho (169)
foiled (170)	suspicious (170)	penlight (172)	cringed (173)
yelps (173)	tentatively (177)	airshaft (177)	

Directions: Select pairs of vocabulary words for each sentence. Then complete the sentence by explaining why the words go together.

Example: *Penlight* and *airshaft* go together because *you might use a penlight to see while walking through an airshaft.*

1. _____ and _____ go together because _____

_____.

2. _____ and _____ go together because _____

_____.

3. _____ and _____ go together because _____

_____.

4. _____ and _____ go together because _____

_____.

5. _____ and _____ go together because _____

_____.

6. _____ and _____ go together because _____

_____.

7. _____ and _____ go together because _____

_____.

whipped (180)	spectacularly (181)	blessedly (182)	precious (182)
wearily (184)	audible (185)	wicker (185)	transport (186)
spokes (186)	grazing (186)	sneered (187)	conscious (190)
deposit (191)	magically (192)	quivered (194)	bared (196)
privilege (197)	brazenly (197)	impression (198)	lurking (198)

Directions: Use three words from the vocabulary list in an original sentence about each of the following characters from the story. Use a different set of words for each character. One word will be used twice.

1. Palmer

2. Dorothy

3. Beans

4. Nipper

5. Farquar

6. Mrs. LaRue

7. Henry

Now rewrite each sentence, but add one more word from the list. Write your new sentences on the back of this paper.

cicada (199)	defenseless (200)	land mine (200)	platoon (200)
deployment (200)	crossfire (200)	fusillade (201)	regrouped (201)
semipro (201)	pureness (202)	macadam (202)	blotting (202)
tension (205)	reconstituted (205)	throttling (205)	intense (210)
pellets (211)	rotated (213)	sarcasm (223)	flexed (224)

Directions: Think about the characters listed below. Write each vocabulary word under the character you associate with that word. One character will have only six words. (There may be more than one way to sort the words. Be prepared to support your decisions about where words belong.)

Palmer	Beans	Dorothy
_____	_____	_____
_____	_____	_____
_____	_____	_____
_____	_____	_____
_____	_____	_____
_____	_____	_____

Sociogram

Directions: A sociogram shows the relationship between characters in a story. Think about Palmer LaRue and his relationships with the characters listed on the sociogram. Complete the sociogram by writing a word to describe the relationship between Palmer and each character. Remember, relationships go both ways, so each line requires a descriptive word. Add other characters to the sociogram and describe the relationship between them and Palmer.

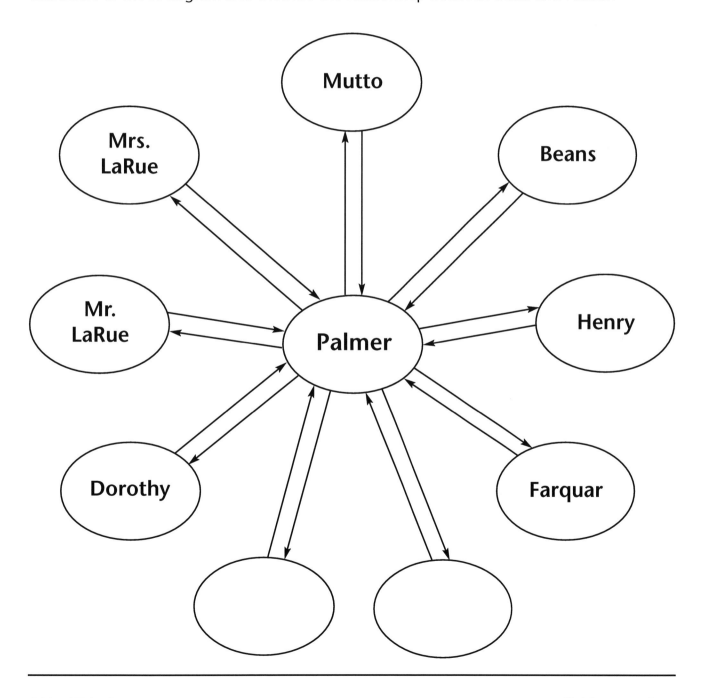

Conflict

The **conflict** of a story is the struggle between two people or two forces. There are three main types of conflict: person against person, person against nature or society, and person against himself/herself.

Directions: The characters in *Wringer* experience some conflicts in the story. In the chart below, list the names of three characters that Palmer must struggle against. In the space provided, list the conflict Palmer experiences with each one and explain how each conflict is resolved in the story.

Character:

Conflict	Resolution

Character:

Conflict	Resolution

Character:

Conflict	Resolution

© Novel Units, Inc.

24

Foreshadowing

Foreshadowing is the literary technique of giving clues to coming events in a story.

Directions: Think about the story *Wringer*. What examples of foreshadowing do you recall from the story? If necessary, scan through the chapters to find examples of foreshadowing. List at least four below. Explain what clues are given and list the coming event that is being suggested.

Foreshadowing	Page #	Clues	Coming Event

Creating Birds from Paper

Directions: Look through some Origami books to find patterns for paper birds. You may want to experiment with several Origami patterns to find the best design for your bird. After you have decided on a design, create your bird from paper. You may use markers, sequins, paint or other art supplies to add color to your bird. Display your bird in the room.

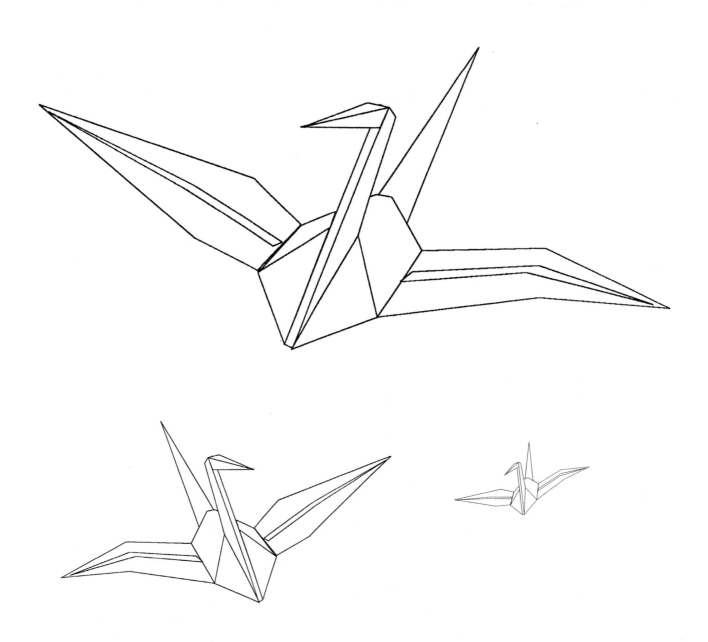

Character Attribute Web

Directions: Think about the characters from *Wringer*. Which character was your favorite? Why? List this character on the attribute web. (You may have made attribute webs for several characters as you read the book. If so, use information recorded from these webs to review the characters and select qualities to list on the attribute web below.) Then use details from the attribute web to write a character sketch of your favorite character.

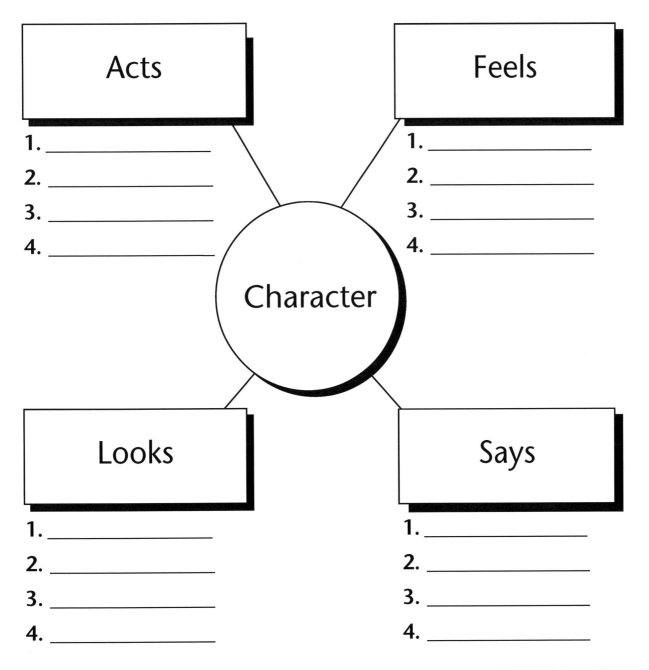

Understanding Values

Directions: Values represent people's beliefs about what is important, good, or worthwhile. For example, most families consider obeying parents very important—it is something they value.

Think about the following characters from *Wringer* and the values they have: Palmer, Dorothy, Beans, Mutto, Henry, and Mrs. LaRue. What do they value? What beliefs do they have about what is important, good, or worthwhile?

On the chart below, list each character's three most important values, from most important to least important. Be prepared to share your lists during a class discussion.

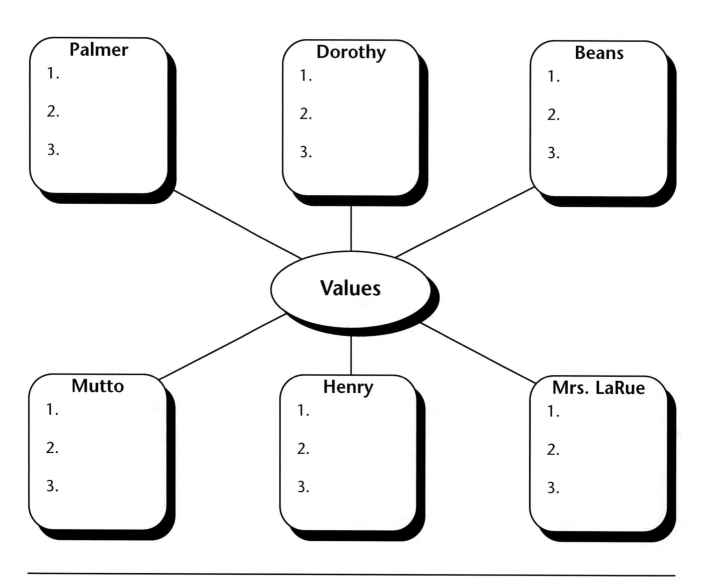

Writing a Riddle

Directions: Write two riddles that describe two different characters in the book, *Wringer*. Be sure to include adjectives, adverbs, nouns, and verbs that will help the other students guess the characters you choose to describe.

_____

_____

_____

_____

_____

_____

_____

_____

_____

_____

_____

_____

_____

_____

Newspaper Article: Extra! Extra!

Directions: A well-written newspaper article always answers the journalist's five questions: who? what? when? where? why? In addition, the article usually goes on to explain HOW the events of the story took place. Pretend you are a news reporter for the Waymer Newspaper. Choose one of the following events from *Wringer* and write an article about it. Remember to answer the journalist's questions and explain how the event happened. Think of an interesting headline for your article and write it on the top line.

Choose one:
- Palmer LaRue turns nine.
- Dorothy Gruzik is harassed by the Beans Boys.
- Palmer saves Nipper at Family Fest.
- Palmer LaRue turns ten.
- Palmer LaRue tickles his teacher.
- Farquar gives a birthday boy The Treatment.

_____

_____

_____

_____

_____

_____

_____

_____

_____

_____

_____

_____

Directions: Mark each statement as either True (T) or False (F). If the statement is false, correct it so that it is true.

_____ 1. Palmer is eager to become a wringer.

_____ 2. Mrs. LaRue is glad Beans, Mutto, and Henry came to Palmer's ninth birthday party.

_____ 3. Palmer feels a sense of pride and honor after receiving The Treatment.

_____ 4. After seeing the pigeons in the big city, Palmer decides they are beautiful.

_____ 5. By the time he turns nine years old, Palmer is excited about Pigeon Day and can't wait to be a wringer.

_____ 6. Palmer finds a pigeon on his snowy window seal.

_____ 7. Palmer is thrilled when a pigeon taps on his window and immediately asks his mother if he can keep it as a pet.

_____ 8. Palmer learns how to care for pigeons by reading a library book.

_____ 9. Palmer uses attacks on Dorothy as a diversion to keep his friends from his house.

_____ 10. Palmer nails a muskrat to Dorothy's door as a joke.

Directions: Write a brief answer (one or two sentences) for each question.

1. How does Palmer react when Mutto sees a pigeon flying near Palmer's house?

2. How does Palmer's relationship with Dorothy change after she confronts him about teasing her?

3. How do Beans' feelings about turning ten differ from Palmer's?

4. How is Henry different from the other boys in the gang?

5. Explain how Palmer's feeling about "floating" in a pool is similar to the way he feels about Dorothy.

6. Why does Palmer start to behave badly at school about a month before summer vacation?

7. What does Dorothy mean when she tells Palmer he is a hero?

8. Why does the gang turn against Palmer?

9. Why does Palmer want to release Nipper into the wild far from his house instead of keeping him or letting Dorothy keep him?

10. How does Palmer's relationship with the gang change after his tenth birthday?

Name _____

Quotations

Directions: Match the name of the character to the correct quotation. Some names may be used more than once or not at all.

A. Palmer	B. Mutto	C. Beans	D. Henry
E. Mrs. LaRue	F. Mr. LaRue	G. Farquar	H. Dorothy

____ 1. "Guess I gotta start yelling then. Fishface! Fishface! Fishface!"

____ 2. "And the nickname, you should hear the nickname they gave him for his ninth birthday, the hoodlums."

____ 3. "Will I be a wringer too?"

____ 4. "Why don't you just blow them up and put them out of their misery all at once?"

____ 5. "How about, besides knocking, if I blow a whistle when I'm on my way?"

____ 6. "Why are you doing this to me?

____ 7. "'Cause I ain't ten till I get The Treatment."

____ 8. "Palmer, be honest, did you really spit on the floor?"

____ 9. "Don't you want to learn how to wring pigeons? Don't you want to learn how to wrrrrring their necks?"

____ 10. "You don't want to be a wringer. You're not going to be a wringer."

____ 11. "No, I don't hate pigeons. Never did."

____ 12. "Take my word for it, that bird is as safe with your dad as it is with you."

Identification: Identify each of the following and explain why each one is important in the story.

    1. Family Fest

    2. Pigeon Day

    3. Nicknames

    4. Tenth birthday

    5. Soccer field

    6. Wringers

    7. Friendship

    8. The Treatment

    9. Treestumping

    10. Nipper

Multiple Choice: Circle the letter for the BEST answer to each question.

    1. What did Palmer receive as gifts from his friends on his ninth birthday?
       A. a frog, a snake, and a piece of string
       B. a marble, a frog, and a stick
       C. a truck, a yo-yo, and a shoe
       D. an apple core, a sock, and a cigar butt

    2. Palmer hates the soccer field in the park because
       A. he doesn't like soccer
       B. it is always muddy
       C. that is where Pigeon Day takes place
       D. there are snakes in that part of the park

3. Palmer receives The Treatment from
   A. Farquar
   B. Beans
   C. Mutto
   D. Henry

4. What does Palmer receive from his father on his ninth birthday?
   A. a frog
   B. toy soldiers
   C. a pet pigeon
   D. a golden pigeon statue

5. Palmer thinks the pigeons he sees in the big city
   A. look like rats and pester people
   B. are mean because they attacked a man in the park
   C. are plump, pretty birds with shiny coats
   D. look filthy and dirty

6. After Palmer finds a pigeon in the snow he
   A. wrings its neck to put it out of misery
   B. feeds the starving pigeon birdseed
   C. feeds the pudgy pigeon FrankenPuffs
   D. hides the bird in a shoebox

7. Palmer learns that pigeons
   A. only eat bugs
   B. live mostly in big cities
   C. have a heart the size of a pea
   D. sleep during the day and are active at night

8. Palmer names his pigeon Nipper because
   A. it is always nipping at something
   B. it was nippy and cold outside when he found it
   C. Dorothy suggests that it would be a good name
   D. that's the brand name written on his basketball

9. What does Beans nail to Dorothy's door as a joke?
   A. a pigeon
   B. a cat
   C. a snake
   D. a muskrat

10. What gifts does Beans get on his tenth birthday?
   A. a muskrat, a pigeon, and a snake
   B. a baseball, a knife, and a can of beans
   C. a book, a card, and a pigeon
   D. a snake, a baseball card, and a football

11. According to Palmer, Dorothy makes him feel the same as when he
   A. has a birthday
   B. is with Nipper
   C. is floating
   D. is sick

12. About a month before the end of school Nipper
   A. lands on Palmer's head as he walks home with the gang
   B. leaves and never returns
   C. shows up at Palmer's house with a broken wing
   D. is stolen by Dorothy to get revenge on Palmer for teasing her

13. What does Palmer do to prompt his teacher to punish him after school?
   A. He pulls Dorothy's hair.
   B. He cheats on a test.
   C. He brings Nipper to school.
   D. He spits on the floor.

14. On the last day of school, Palmer
   A. spits on the floor
   B. wears an elephant mask
   C. stays home sick
   D. confesses to his teacher that he has a pigeon

15. Why does Palmer hide behind the sofa the night of his birthday?
   A. Beans, Mutto, and Henry will mess up his bedroom if they come through his bedroom window.
   B. He doesn't want the gang to know that he is Dorothy's friend.
   C. If the gang comes into his room they will find Nipper, his pet pigeon.
   D. His mother and father do not like Beans and will not let Palmer invite him to the house.

16. Where do Palmer and Dorothy take Nipper to release him?
   A. the meadow
   B. the woods
   C. the seashore
   D. behind the GreatGrocer

17. Palmer saves Nipper by
   A. setting him free in the city
   B. keeping him in a cage until Pigeon Day is over
   C. donating him to a bird sanctuary at the zoo
   D. running onto the soccer field and grabbing him before he is shot

I. Analysis (Choose A or B)

   A. Think about Palmer, the main character from the story. How does Palmer change during the story? Does he change for the better or the worse? Write a composition (two paragraphs minimum) that explains how Palmer changes and whether these changes are for the better or the worse. Use information from the story to support your answer.

   B. Think about events that happen in *Wringer*. How does one event sometimes cause another? Choose an event from the story and write a brief composition (one or two paragraphs) that explains how this event caused other events to happen. Use information from the story to support your answer.

II. Creative Writing (Choose A or B)

   A. Pretend that you are Palmer. Write five journal entries about some of the events that happen to you on your way to and from school.

   B. Dorothy tells Palmer, "You're a hero...You're probably the naughtiest student there's ever been in our school. And you're doing it all to save him" (p. 149). Think about a time when you were faced with peer pressure and had to choose between doing what was right and what your friends wanted you to do. Think about how it made you feel and how your friends reacted. Write a letter or poem about your experience describing how it affected you. You could even write about your experience in the form of a short anecdote using dialogue.

Answer Key

Activities #1 and #2: Answers will vary.

Study Questions—Section One: Chapters 1-4: 1. He does not want to be a wringer. 2. The moment when not wanting to be a wringer turns into becoming one. 3. A boy who breaks the neck of the wounded pigeons and places the bodies in bags during the shooting on Pigeon Day. 4. He scoops the icing off with his finger. 5. Beans. 6. A cigar butt, a rotten apple core, and an old sock. 7. Snots. 8. Henry. 9. Dorothy Gruzik. 10. A bag of mud and sticks; dog poop. 11. He hates the park. The soccer field is where Pigeon Day takes place. 12. He says his leg hurts. 13. Henry. 14. Pigeon Day three years earlier. **Section Two: Chapters 5-8:** 1. Diving head first down the sliding board. 2. Slide down headfirst, all four stacked. 3. He clamps the sides halfway down and stops, sending the rest of the boys tumbling to the ground. 4. He pinches his nose and yells, "Ehh, yer old man!" 5. A legendary wringer and the coolest, most feared kid in town. 6. The Treatment is the ultimate test and honor where a child receives mistreatment on his birthday. Palmer receives nine knuckle punches in the arm from Farquar. 7. They grin while watching. 8. He thinks Beans is a "pip" and Mrs. LaRue thinks he is a hoodlum. 9. From his love for cold baked beans out of a can, anytime, day or night. 10. Twenty-seven toy soldiers. 11. On the high shelf of his closet. 12. He keeps busy by reading a book, watching TV, inspecting his presents, and thinking about the day. 13. Brushing his teeth. 14. No; He doesn't want the attention to end. 15. She ignores him. 16. She does not look at them, say anything to them, run away, or cry. 17. The first Saturday in August; it's Pigeon Day. 18. He wonders why anyone would pay for a pigeon just to shoot it. 19. Four years old. 20. In honor of all pigeons; this house loves you. 21. Yes. 22. Yes. **Section Three: Chapters 9-12:** 1. Dorothy and her family. 2. Dorothy. 3. She runs away from Palmer and the Pigeon Day crowd. 4. Beans. 5. Swinging. 6. He wraps it in newspaper and hides it under his bed, then he charges other kids a quarter to look at it. 7. The gray and sour odor of gun smoke. 8.Mutto. 9. He is too small, too young, he has a funny name, and he plays with little girls. 10. She drags Dorothy to the party. 11. Pigeons nod their heads as they walk. 12. He reads the inscription on the pigeon statue in the den. 13. On his second Pigeon Day, when he sat with Dorothy on the swings. 14. To raise money for the park. 15. He is going to pretend he is sick. 16. Beans and Mutto. 17. They go to the railroad station where the pigeons awaiting the shoot are kept. 18. He stays in bed and pretends to be sick. **Section Four: Chapters 13-16:** 1. It rains. 2. There is a blizzard. 3. He rides his sled down Valentine's Hill all day with Beans, Mutto, and Henry. 4. A pigeon. 5. Dorothy. 6. Yes. 7. The bird is hungry. 8. FrankenPuffs. 9. It walks in like a person with its head bobbing, acting cool. 10. Scratchy-good. 11. No, it is pudgy. 12. She casually shrugs and says, "Okay." 13. To give Palmer time to cover himself up because he is getting too old for his mother to see him in his underwear. **Section Five: Chapters 17-20:** 1. It pinches his earlobe. 2. Grape Nuts. 3. No. 4. A book about pigeons 5. That's what it is called when a bird goes to sleep as soon as the sun goes down. 6. It's okay to feed a pigeon cereal; sometimes pigeons eat gravel to help breakdown food; they have no teeth; they aren't fussy about what they eat; they only have thirty-seven taste buds. 7.Measured against the size of its body, it is one of the largest hearts in creation. 8. The bird is always nipping at something. 9. Acting normal. 10. He offers to change his own bed sheets from now on. 11. He wants to keep the boys away from his house so they do not find Nipper. 12. Standing in front of Dorothy as she walks home so she has to keep walking around the gang. 13. A lean-to, cave, or hole 14. A nice, regular house. 15. A dead muskrat.16. Tree bark or sewer grate flotsam 17. From Panther, his cat. 18. Panther is the meanest cat in town and is always killing things and leaving them on the front steps like a present. 19. He nails it to the Gruziks' front door and rings the bell. 20. Mrs. Gruzik. 21. A pigeon. **Section Six: Chapters 21-24:** 1. A pigeon. 2. He tells his friends he is treating at the deli. 3. The muskrat carcass, the scream, and the pigeon sighting. 4. He grabs Nipper and pulls him in, then rubs his tear-streaked face against Nipper. 5. Fly around town, go to the park, steer clear of the soccer field, and fly to other towns. 6. That Nipper would fly to another boy in another town so Nipper would be safe. 7. They stay away from her house but continue to torment her on the way to and from school. 8. The other boys and girls start treestumping each other. 9. A red hat. 10. She breaks her silence as Beans is tormenting her by walking over to Palmer and asking, "Why are you doing this to me?" 11. Palmer. 12. He gets very upset. He cries, can't eat his dinner, and has trouble falling asleep. 13. Dorothy. 14. A baseball from Palmer, pocket knife from Henry, and Campbells' baked beans from Mutto. 15. He doesn't consider himself to be ten until he gets The Treatment. 16. No. 17. That's the nickname for Beans, Henry, Mutto, and Palmer. 18. She puts a piece of cotton in her ear. 19. Floating. 20. He does not want to be a wringer. 21. She tells him if he doesn't want to be a wringer then he shouldn't be a wringer. 22. He thinks Beans will wring his neck. 23. First he is stunned, and then he laughs. **Section Seven: Chapters 25-28:** 1. Nipper lands on his head as he is walking with his friends. 2. He pretends to chase after Nipper and denies that Nipper is his pet. 3. He claims to hate them. 4. Kill pigeons. 5. Nipper's Ball. 6. He dresses in his winter clothes. 7. Spit on the floor. 8. He must write on the blackboard one hundred times, "I will never spit on the floor again." 9. His mom made him because she thinks he is getting the flu. 10. Henry. 11. How to avoid Nipper on the way home from

school and how to keep the guys from turning against him. 12. He gets into trouble at school. 13. Puberty. 14. He tickles the teacher. 15. An elephant mask. His teacher is not going to keep him after school on the last day, and he needs a disguise. 16. Wringer school. 17. Neon pink. 18. Five. 19. Fast. 20. Wounded birds that need to be killed. 21. It's the next Pigeon Day. **Section Eight: Chapters 29-32:** 1.They were playing with a foamy basketball. 2. Dorothy tells Palmer to tell everybody that he doesn't want to be a wringer. 3. Palmer's social life is divided into two separate relationships: one with Dorothy, and one with the guys. 4. Palmer is trying to stay on the guys' good side. 5. His wish is to go to bed and not wake up until September. 6. She sees the cat around the house and inside on the stairway. 7. Palmer's father's Sharpshooter Award. 8. He sees the ghosts of ten pigeons. 9. No, the boys cannot find Farquar. 10. He finds the word "tonight" written in the icing. 11. He goes upstairs three times during the party. 12. He decides to go downstairs and hide in the dark behind the sofa. 13. Nipper goes into a dopey trance that firecrackers could not disturb. 14. Palmer forgets to bring the Honey Crunchers, Nipper's food, downstairs. 15. Beans rings the doorbell. 16. Palmer tells the gang that he spent the night with his cousin. 17. Beans tells Palmer that they must go find Farquar. 18. Farquar is eating a cupcake and drinking a Coke. 19. Palmer says, "No, nothing! No Treatment! No wringer! No Snots!" 20. Palmer runs away down the street as the gang runs after him. **Section Nine: Chapters 33-36:** 1. He hides near a dumpster behind the GreatGrocer supermarket. 2. The worker gives Palmer a can of Sprite. 3. Palmer runs for home as the sun drops below the roofline of the GreatGrocer. 4. The yellow cat, Panther, is sitting on Palmer's bed. 5. At her house. 6. No, because they really love Nipper but don't want to see him dead. 7. She finds the unflattenable Nerf ball. 8. They take a box of donuts and mini-cartons of iced tea. 9. She feeds him a piece of donut. 10. He releases him in the woods next to a meadow. 11. They buy sodas. 12. They find Nipper waiting for them on the windowsill. 13. Palmer's mother. 14. His mother tells Palmer that she and his father know about Nipper. 15. She uses a tissue. 16. She and her parents are going to the seashore. 17. Palmer asks Dorothy to take Nipper with her and let him go by the seashore. 18. Henry. 19. His real name is George. 20. Palmer tells Henry to say that he wants to quit the gang. **Section Ten: Chapters 37-40:** 1. He rides his bike down empty alleyways. 2. Palmer keeps his soldiers in his sock drawer. 3. Palmer's father teaches him the proper placement of the troops. 4. Palmer buries the soldiers in the backyard. 5. They go to Denville. 6. Mr. LaRue catches a foul ball and gives it to Palmer. 7. Palmer imagines he feels a heartbeat. 8. The women are baking pies and the men are cleaning their shotguns. 9. Palmer dreams that a pigeon is run over by a car and when he is brought back to life a wringer is throttling the pigeon. 10. Palmer's favorite pie is raspberry crumb. 11. Mr. LaRue walks right past the shooting gallery. 12. He rides it to the old train station. 13. He finds stacks of crates filled with pigeons. 14. Five birds. 16. Beans and Mutto wring the pigeons' necks and Henry carries the white boxes. 17. Dorothy. 18. Dorothy tells Palmer she let Nipper go out the window at the railroad yards. 19. Dorothy runs away screaming because she learns that Nipper may be one of the pigeons being shot during the Family Fest. 20. A workman. 21. The shooter fires at a Frisbee that is thrown out onto the field. 22. Palmer meets a seven-year-old boy. 23. Beans. 24. Yes.
Activities #3 and #4: Answers will vary. **Activity #5:** 1. yanked (s) 2. nuisance (a) 3. uproar (s) 4. intended (s) 5. fiery (a) 6. wobbled (s) 7. dashing (s) 8. strutted (a) 9. misery (a) 10. wrenching (s)
Activities 6-20: Answers will vary.
Comprehension Quiz #1: 1. F 2. F 3. T 4. T 5. F 6. T 7. F 8. T 9. T 10. F
Comprehension Quiz #2: 1. He tries to distract the gang so they won't find Nipper. 2. He begins to see her as a person he has hurt deeply and then renews their friendship. 3. Beans wants to turn ten so he can be a wringer. Palmer dreads turning ten because he does not want to be a wringer. 4. He is the tallest and the meekest. Henry is nice when he warns Palmer about Beans coming to visit him and takes care of his own little sister. 5. He knows that he can let go and she will hold him up. He knows he can trust her with his secrets. 6. He wants to stay after school so he will avoid seeing Nipper on the way home. He also wants to boost his popularity with his friends so they will not turn against him because of Nipper. 7. She thinks he is a hero because he is getting into trouble at school to save Nipper. 8. He refuses The Treatment, tells the gang he doesn't want to be a wringer, and says his name is Palmer not Snots. In addition, the gang believes Palmer has a pet pigeon. 9. He thinks the gang will kill Nipper if the bird stays in town. He wants to release Nipper far from his house so Nipper won't be able to find his way back. 10. The gang turns on Palmer and no longer considers him their friend. They harass and tease Palmer whenever they see him.
Novel Test—Quotations: 1. C 2. E 3. A 4. A 5. E 6. H 7. C 8. D 9. C 10. H 11. F 12. E
Identification: Answers will vary.
Multiple Choice: 1. D 2. C 3. A 4. B 5. C 6. C 7. B 8. A 9. D 10. B 11. C 12. A 13. D 14. B 15. C 16. B 17. D
Essays: Use rubric on following page to evaluate student compositions.

Essay Evaluation Form

This evaluation is designed to help the teacher assess a student's essay on a 100-point scale. Circle one number (excellent/good/needs improvement) per category to get the total grade.

	Excellent	Good	Needs Improvement
1. **Focus:** The student writes a clear thesis and includes it in the opening paragraph.	10	8	4
2. **Organization:** The final draft reflects the assigned outline; transitions are used to link ideas.	20	16	12
3. **Support:** Adequate details are provided; extraneous details are omitted.	12	10	7
4. **Detail:** Each quote or reference is explained (as if the teacher had not read the book); ideas are not redundant.	12	10	7
5. **Mechanics:** Spelling, capitalization, and usage are correct.	16	12	8
6. **Sentence Structure:** The student avoids run-ons and sentence fragments.	10	8	4
7. **Verb:** All verbs are in the correct tense; sections in which plot is summarized are in the present tense.	10	8	4
8. **Total effect of the essay**	10	8	4

Comments:

Total: _____

(This rubric may be altered to fit the needs of a particular class. You may wish to show it to students before they write their essays. They can use it as a self-evaluation tool, and they will be aware of exactly how their essays will be graded.)
